SUPER SPORTS STAR

EDDIE GEORGE

Stew Thornley

Enslow Publishers, Inc.

40 Industrial Road   PO Box 38
Box 398   Aldershot
Berkeley Heights, NJ 07922 Hants GU12 6BP
USA   UK

http://www.enslow.com

Library of Congress Cataloging-in-Publication Data

Thornley, Stew.
    Super sports star Eddie George / Stew Thornley.
        p. cm. — (Super sports star)
    Summary: Profiles running back Eddie George of the Tennessee Titans, who helped to bring his team to the 1999 AFC championship game with a sixty-eight yard run for a touchdown.
    Includes bibliographical references (p.   ) and index.
    ISBN 0-7660-2050-9
    1. George, Eddie, 1973—-Juvenile literature. 2. Football players—United States—Biography—Juvenile literature. [1. George, Eddie, 1973- 2. Football players. 3. African Americans—Biography.] I. Title. II. Series.
    GV939.G46 T56 2003
    796.332'092—dc21   2002004247

Printed in the United States of America

10 9 8 7 6 5 4 3 2 1

To Our Readers:
We have done our best to make sure all Internet Addresses in this book were active and appropriate when we went to press. However, the author and the publisher have no control over and assume no liability for the material available on those Internet sites or on other Web sites they may link to. Any comments or suggestions can be sent by e-mail to comments@enslow.com or to the address on the back cover.

Photo Credits: © James Biever/NFL Photos, p. 4; © Mary Ann Carter/NFL Photos, p. 33; © David Drapkin/NFL Photos, p. 21; © Glenn James/NFL Photos, p. 19; © Allen Kee/NFL Photos, p. 6; © G. Newman Lowrance/NFL Photos, pp. 8, 25; © Darrell McAllister/NFL Photos, pp. 16, 23; © Al Messerschmidt/NFL Photos, p. 29; © Marty Morrow/NFL Photos, pp. 1, 9, 12, 14, 31, 44; © Al Pereira/NFL Photos, pp. 34, 36; © Joe Robbins/NFL Photos, pp. 11, 38, 39; © Tony Tomsic/NFL Photos, p. 27.

Cover Photo: © Marty Morrow/NFL Photos.

CONTENTS

Running backs have to be tough. Eddie George is one of the toughest.

Introduction

Eddie George is a running back for the Tennessee Titans. He is one of the best runners in the National Football League (NFL).

Running backs get tackled a lot. They have to be tough or they will not last long. They have huge 350-pound linemen or bruising linebackers crashing into them.

Eddie George does most of the running for the Titans. He often leads the NFL in the number of times he carries the ball. George takes a lot of hits, but he also gives them back.

George is one of the most rugged runners in the league. Miami linebacker Zach Thomas once said, "The problem with him is he would sometimes run into you rather than run around you."

No wonder Eddie George's nickname is "The Beast."

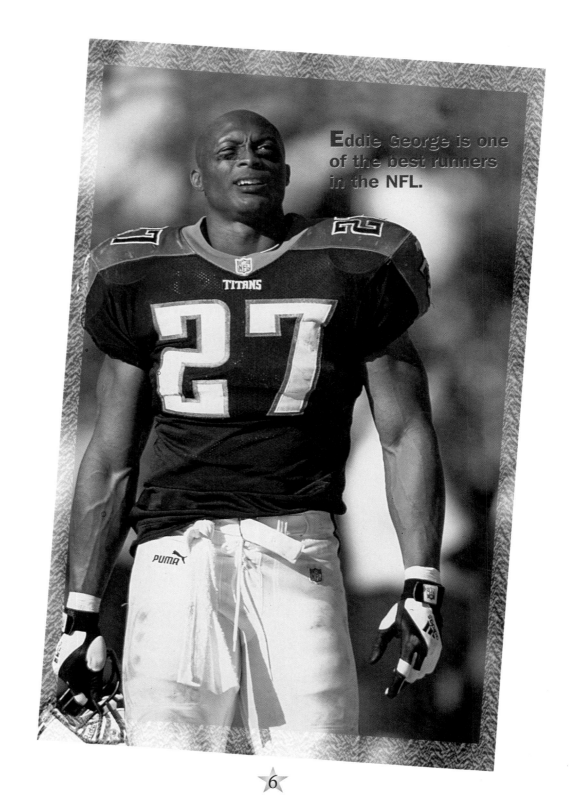

Eddie George is one of the best runners in the NFL.

George helps the Titans in many ways. Opposing defenses have to watch him closely. That makes it easier for the Titans to pass the ball. As George grinds out yards running the ball, it keeps the Tennessee offense on the field. That means the team's defense gets to rest more. That is another way George helps his team.

The Titans would hate to be without George. They never are, though. George gets banged up when he plays. But because he is in great shape, he has never missed a game in the NFL.

When he was in college, his coach said, "Nobody could have a better work ethic than Eddie George." His hard work pays off. It helps him to stay healthy and keep playing.

George knows what his job is. "I'm supposed to get the hard, tough yards," he says. "That's why I play this game. I've been playing this game for quite a while now, and I know what to expect out of my body and how I'm going to feel after the game. And I hope I've dished out some punishment, as well."

Eddie George is a real Titan.

Eddie George runs with the ball.

Taking the Titans to the Top

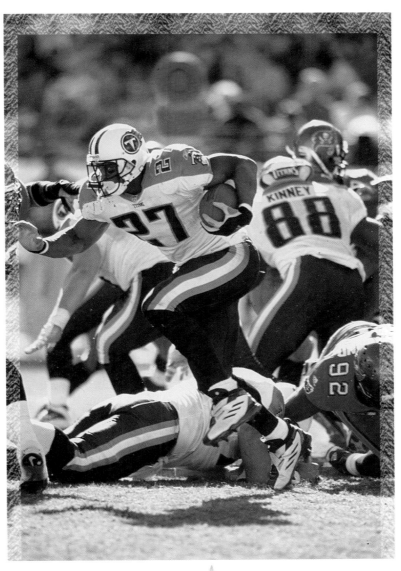

The Tennessee Titans made the playoffs in 1999. They won their first game. Next, they played the Indianapolis Colts in Indianapolis, Indiana. The winner would go to the American Football Conference (AFC) championship game.

The game started out as a defensive battle. Indianapolis held Eddie George to 38 yards rushing in the first half. He did not score a touchdown. Al Del Greco kicked two field goals for Tennessee. But the Indianapolis kicker booted three through the goal posts. At the end of the first half, the Colts led by a score of 9–6.

Tennessee got the ball to start the second half. They were in their own territory. The Colts expected a pass. They put on a strong rush against quarterback Steve McNair. McNair did not pass. He handed off to Eddie George.

George took the ball and took a step to his left. Then he stopped and went the other direction. The big pass rush left a gap in the Colts' line. George spotted the hole and headed toward it. He put on a burst of speed and sailed through. George broke into the open and kept going.

By the time he stopped, he was in the end zone. His 68-yard run put the Titans ahead. It was the only touchdown of the day for Tennessee. Del Greco kicked two more field goals in the fourth quarter. By the time the Colts got a touchdown, it was too late.

George had a great day. He rushed for a total of 162 yards. Tennessee won the game, 19–16. The Titans were going to the AFC championship game, and Eddie George was leading the way.

Eddie George helped the Tennessee Titans go to the AFC championship game.

Getting Back on Track

Eddie George was born on September 24, 1973 and grew up in Philadelphia, Pennsylvania. Eddie's parents were divorced when he was five-years-old. Donna George worked hard to raise Eddie and his sister, Leslie. She often worked two jobs. Eddie and Leslie stayed with their grandmother while their mom was working.

George played soccer, basketball, and baseball. "[T]hose other sports are cool, but I needed something more physical," George said. But his mom thought he was too small to play football. She was afraid he would get hurt.

George's friends were playing football, and he wanted to play, too. He tried to talk his mom into changing her mind. He behaved as well as he could. He did the dishes, cleaned his room,

Eddie George played
many sports as a kid,
but he really wanted
to play football.

and took out the trash. He was hoping his mom would give him a break. At last, she did.

George loved carrying the ball. He told his mom, "I want to go to college on a football scholarship. I want to win the Heisman and then after that, go to the pros."

The Heisman Trophy is awarded to the best college football player each season. George practiced speeches of what he would say if he won the award.

George went to Abington High School in Philadelphia. He played football and was also on the track team. On weekends, George sold hot chocolate at Veterans Stadium. That is where the Philadelphia Eagles play. George hoped someday he would play at Veterans Stadium.

But George started hanging out with a bad crowd. He stopped trying hard in school. He was headed for trouble.

His mom was worried. She knew that Eddie needed to get back on track.

To do that, she sent him to a military school

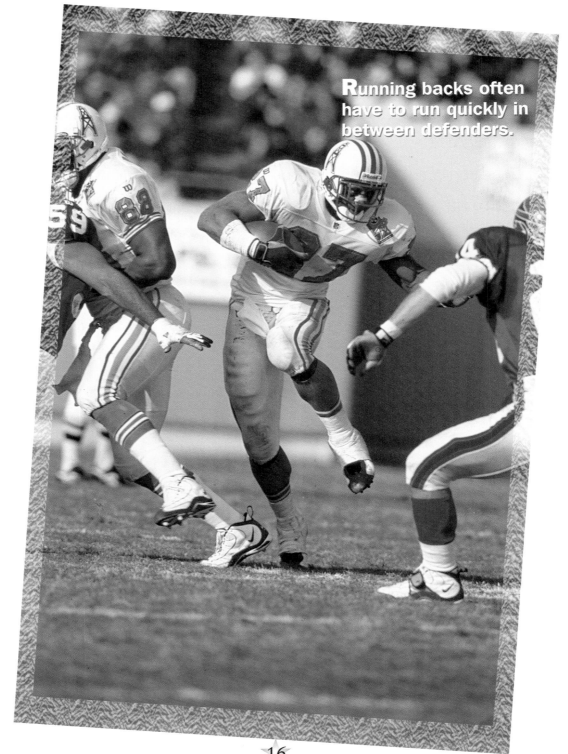

Running backs often have to run quickly in between defenders.

in Virginia. George started his junior year of high school at Fork Union Military Academy. He was not happy about it because the school had many rules. But George followed the rules. If he did not, he would not be allowed to play football.

George got up at 6:00 each morning. He had chores to do and classes to attend. Then he had football practice. George worked hard at all these things. He asked Mickey Sullivan, the football coach, what he would have to do to be a star in football. Sullivan worked out a conditioning program. George lifted weights. He spent time on the running track. He got stronger and faster. "He did everything he had to do," said Sullivan.

George had a great football career at Fork Union. He scored thirty-two touchdowns in his two years there. He was captain of the team when he was a senior. George was also on the track team. He won the state title in the high hurdles and low hurdles.

George's mother had been worried about her decision to send her son away to school. She thought he might hate her for doing it. But George understood why his mother did this. "I was hardheaded, and I didn't listen," he said.

The first time Donna George went to visit Eddie at Fork Union, she did not know how he would react. She arrived during a military drill. Eddie was in the front row. He was sharply dressed and holding a flag. George spotted his mother in the crowd. He smiled at her. Donna George was happy to see her son.

"It instilled discipline in me," George said later, of the time at Fork Union.

For Eddie George, that changed his life.

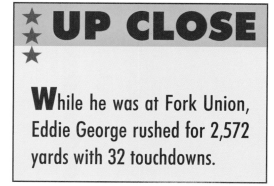

★★ **UP CLOSE**
★

While he was at Fork Union, Eddie George rushed for 2,572 yards with 32 touchdowns.

Go Eddie!

Eddie George went to college at Ohio State University. Ohio State has a great football program. George played football for the Ohio State Buckeyes.

He majored in landscape architecture. A landscape architect learns how to take care of the environment. They also decide where plants and trees should go to make a good outdoor space, like a park.

On campus at Ohio State is an area called Buckeye Grove. A tree is planted in honor of every player who makes the All-America team. As George walked through the grove for the first time, he said to himself, "I want a Buckeye Tree."

It took him a while to get going. The Buckeyes already had some good running backs. George did not play much when he was a freshman or sophomore. When he did play, things did not go well.

Once when he was a freshman, he had a terrible afternoon. He fumbled twice near the

Even in the snow,
Eddie George can
run the ball.

goal line. As a result, Ohio State lost to the University of Illinois. As George ran off the field, he was booed.

George's mom was waiting for him when he came out of the locker room. She walked him back into the stadium. "Now you sit and cry," she said to her son. "And when you walk out of this stadium, you walk with your head up."

George started playing regularly when he was a junior. He ran for more than 1,400 yards and twelve touchdowns. He ran for 206 yards against Northwestern University. He ran for 219 yards against Michigan State University. That was the first time a Buckeye had ever run for more than 200 yards twice in the same season.

George had a great year as a junior. But he was just warming up.

The Buckeyes opened their 1995 season with a game called the Kickoff Classic, which was played in New Jersey. Ohio State played against Boston College. George rushed for 99 yards and two touchdowns. He was named the Most Valuable Player (MVP) of the Kickoff Classic. It was the last time that season he was held to fewer than 100 yards.

The Buckeyes kept winning, and George kept doing well. Ohio State was undefeated through the end of October.

By this time, George was in the running for the Heisman Trophy. It was the award he often dreamed about as a kid. But now he did not even think about it.

Eddie George wanted his own Buckeye tree in Ohio State's Buckeye Grove.

He wanted to help his team win the Big Ten title. That would put the Buckeyes in the Rose Bowl.

On the first Saturday in November, Ohio State beat the University of Minnesota. George had an 87-yard touchdown run in the game.

The next week, the Buckeyes faced Illinois, the team that George had that terrible game against when he was a freshman. This time, things were different. One of the people watching the game was Archie Griffin. Griffin was the last Ohio State player to win the Heisman Trophy. Every time George got the ball, Griffin leaned forward and chanted, "Go Eddie, Go Eddie, Go Eddie . . . " And did Eddie ever go. He went through the Illinois line. He went around the line. He went through tacklers. When he was done, George had run 314 yards.

No Buckeye had ever run for so many yards in a single game. Eddie George finished the regular season with more than 1,800 yards.

By October of the 1995 season, Eddie George was in the running for a Heisman Trophy.

He ran for twenty-three touchdowns. Three times during the year, he was named the Player of the Week in the Big Ten.

Ohio State lost its final game against the University of Michigan. Instead of going to the Rose Bowl, the Buckeyes went to the Citrus Bowl. George rushed for 101 yards. But the Buckeyes lost to the University of Tennessee, 20–14. It was George's final college game.

George had a great college career. He won the Heisman Trophy and was named to the All-America team. A tree was planted for him in Buckeye Grove.

After the college season ended, George had the chance to go watch the Super Bowl. He saw the Dallas Cowboys and the Pittsburgh Steelers battle for the championship. It was fun to watch. But he wanted to do more than just that.

"I'm going to be playing in this game one day soon," said George.

A Rapid Rookie

Every year the NFL holds a draft in which teams take turns picking the best college players. Eddie George was the fourteenth player taken in the draft. He was chosen by the Houston Oilers.

The Oilers had never played in the Super Bowl. They hoped a great runner like George could help them get there. It did not take long for George to show his ability.

In the second game of the 1996 season, Houston played the Jacksonville Jaguars. The Oilers had the lead in the third quarter. But they were deep in their own territory. George took a handoff and almost got tackled, but he slipped away. He finally got stopped at Jacksonville's 13-yard line. It was a 76-yard gain. George's run set up another touchdown for the Oilers. They went on to win. George had 143 yards rushing in the game.

During Eddie George's first year in the NFL, he was named Rookie of the Year.

George did not get a touchdown himself for a few more weeks. The Oilers trailed the Cincinnati Bengals by ten points. George closed the gap with a 45-yard run into the end zone. Houston won the game in overtime. George finished with 152 yards.

With George playing well, the Oilers were winning games. Houston moved into first place with a win over Pittsburgh. George scored a touchdown late in that game.

The Oilers went into a slump after that. But George finished the season with 1,368 yards rushing. That is a great total for a player in his first year. He also scored eight touchdowns.

George was named the NFL's Rookie of the Year. The Oilers ended the season with an 8–8 record. That was not good enough to get into the playoffs.

The Oilers had a ways to go. But they knew they had the right player to do it with.

A Super Season

The Oilers had a new home in 1997. The team moved to Tennessee, but they did not do any better. Once again, they were 8–8. But George kept playing well. He rushed for nearly 1,400 yards and earned a spot in the Pro Bowl. The Pro Bowl is the NFL's version of an all-star game. Only the top players in the league go to the Pro Bowl.

George played in the Pro Bowl again after the 1998 season. He was doing very well.

The team had a new name in 1999. The name Oilers fit when they were in Texas. In Tennessee, it did not. So the Houston Oilers became the Tennessee Titans.

The Titans had a winning pattern. They won their first three games of the season. After losing one, they won three more. Another loss was followed by three more wins. They lost again. But then they won their last four games.

Tennessee finished the regular season with a record of 13–3. One of the reasons for the great year was Eddie George. He was always a great runner. But now he was becoming a better player. Besides carrying the ball, he could also catch it. George finished the season with thirteen touchdowns. Four were on passes he caught. He also ran the ball well. He had 1,304 yards rushing.

The Titans made it to the playoffs. Their first game was against Buffalo. George ran for 106 yards. They won the game, 22–16, when Kevin Dyson ran back a kickoff for a touchdown.

Eddie George and the Titans made it to the AFC playoffs in 1999.

Next, the Titans played Indianapolis. George had another big game as Tennessee won, 19–16. That put them in the AFC title game. It was against the Jacksonville Jaguars. The Jaguars were the only team in the AFC with a better record than Tennessee during the 1999 season. But the Titans were too good for the Jaguars in this game. Tennessee won, 33–14.

The Titans were going to the Super Bowl. They played the St. Louis Rams in the big game. St. Louis got off to a 16–0 lead. But Tennessee fought back. They trailed 16–6 in the fourth quarter. The Titans had the ball two yards away from the end zone. They

The Titans went to Super Bowl XXXIV.

needed a touchdown. George was the man to get them there.

George took the handoff. He followed a block by his fullback. He crashed through two tacklers. Only a big linebacker stood in his way. George lowered his shoulder and ran past for a touchdown. It was not a long run, but it was a tough one. And it was a big touchdown. It put the Titans within three points of the Rams. Soon after, the teams were tied.

But St. Louis came back with a touchdown. The Rams then held off a final drive. They stopped Tennessee only a yard away from a touchdown that could have tied the game. The Titans lost the game, but they had had a great year.

★★★ **UP CLOSE**

Eddie George has appeared in a few television shows. He has even been in a few commercials.

Success On
and Off the Field

In 2000, Eddie George had his best season ever. He rushed for 1,509 yards, his highest total yet. He also became only the second player ever to run for more than 1,200 yards in each of his first four seasons. The other was Eric Dickerson. He is in the Pro Football Hall of Fame.

One of George's big games came against the Philadelphia Eagles. The game was in Philadelphia, where he had grown up. Many of George's family and friends were in the stands to watch him. George ran for 101 yards. But it was the Tennessee kicker, Al Del Greco, who won the game with a 50-yard field goal on the final play. "We believe we'll find a way to win, even in the final minute," George said after the game. "We never give up or lose our edge. It's not over until the last second."

Tennessee finished first in the AFC Central Division. The Titans opened the playoffs against the Baltimore Ravens. George scored a touchdown on the first drive of the game to put his team ahead. But Baltimore came back and won the game. The Titans' season was over.

After the season, George had surgery to repair a tendon in his right foot. He worked hard in the off-season to make sure he would be ready to play when the next season started. He had never missed a game with the Titans. He did not miss any in 2001. However, he did struggle with injuries. A sprained ankle slowed him down for a few weeks. Even though he played in every game, he was not always in top form.

George had only one game in which he ran for more than 100 yards. It came

In 2000, the Tennessee Titans finished first in the AFC Central Division.

Eddie George knows that getting an education is important. He went back to Ohio State and received his degree in June 2001.

against Cleveland, in the next-to-last game of the season. Tennessee lost that game. The Titans lost a lot of games that year. They finished with a record of 7 wins and 9 losses. The last time the team had a losing record was in 1995, the year before George joined them.

Eddie George does not like losing. He set his sights on the 2002 season. He would do everything he could to make sure that both he and the Titans do better.

A lot of players rest when the season is over. Eddie George does that, too. One thing he likes to do is play video games. But he also works hard during the off-season. He stays in shape so he will be ready for the next season.

★★★ UP CLOSE

Eddie George became the first running back in league history who carried the ball at least 300 times in each of his first five seasons.

George has also worked hard in school. When he left Ohio State to play in the NFL, he had not received his degree. Sometimes athletes leave college without graduating to play professional sports. Some do not finish their studies, but others do. Soon after the Titans played in the Super Bowl in 2000, Eddie George was back at Ohio State. "I couldn't leave something like that undone," he said. "I could have been doing other things this off-season—going to different events and parties—but I made the commitment and sacrifices to finish this so that I can use it down the line for after football." He completed half of his remaining course work after that spring. After the 2001 season, George went back again and completed the rest of his studies. On June 8, 2001, he received his degree in landscape architecture from Ohio State.

He carried his four-year-old son, Jaire, with him as he picked up his diploma. George wanted to set an example for his son, as well as other young people, about how important education is.

"I think it can inspire kids to go back to school. I am in a position where I don't have to go back, but I am the type of person that if I start something I want to finish it. By gaining a degree, it doesn't ensure you will be successful, but it shows a willingness and a persistence that you have to have to finish anything."

CAREER STATISTICS

NFL						
Rushing						
Year	Team	GP	Att.	Yds.	Avg.	TDs
1996	Tennessee	16	335	1,368	4.1	8
1997	Tennessee	16	357	1,399	3.9	6
1998	Tennessee	16	348	1,294	3.7	5
1999	Tennessee	16	320	1,304	4.1	9
2000	Tennessee	16	403	1,509	3.7	14
2001	Tennessee	16	315	939	3.0	5
Totals		96	2,078	7,813	3.8	47

Receiving						
Year	Team	GP	Rec.	Yds.	Avg.	TDs
1996	Tennessee	16	23	182	7.9	0
1997	Tennessee	16	7	44	6.3	1
1998	Tennessee	16	37	310	8.4	1
1999	Tennessee	16	47	458	9.7	4
2000	Tennessee	16	50	453	9.1	2
2001	Tennessee	16	37	279	7.5	0
Totals		96	201	1,726	8.6	8

GP–Games Played   **Yds.**–Yards   **Avg.**–Average
GS–Games Started   **TDs**–Touchdown Passes
Att.–Attempts   **Rec.**–Receptions

Where to Write to Eddie George

Mr. Eddie George
c/o Tennessee Titans
460 Great Circle Road
Nashville, Tennessee 37228

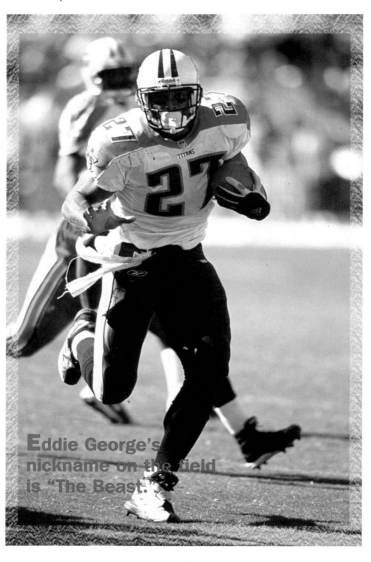

Eddie George's
nickname on the field
is "The Beast."

WORDS TO KNOW

draft—A selection of players by teams, who take turns choosing the players they want.

freshman—A ninth-grade student in high school or a first-year student in college.

fullback—The fullback is normally called upon whenever short yardage is needed. He is usually the most powerful runner on the team. He can drive straight ahead into the line or block for other runners.

Heisman Trophy—The award that is given each year to the best college football player in America.

junior—An eleventh-grade student in high school or a third-year student in college.

quarterback—He is in charge of the offense. He calls the plays, sometimes with help from the bench. The quarterback can either pass the ball, hand it off to a running back, or keep it and run.

rookie—A player in his first full season in professional sports.

scholarship—An award that allows a player to attend college for free.

senior—A twelfth-grade student in high school or a fourth-year student in college.

sophomore—A tenth-grade student in high school or a second-year student in college.

Super Bowl—The NFL's championship game.

READING ABOUT

Books

Dorling Kindersley Publishing Staff. *Play Football!* New York, NY: Dorling Kindersley Publishing, Inc., 2002.

Nelson, Julie. *Tennessee Titans.* Mankato, Minn.: The Creative Company, 2000.

Internet Addresses

The Official Web Site of the Tennessee Titans
    <http://www.titansonline.com/>

Eddie George on NFL.com
    <http://www.nfl.com/players/
    playerpage/1174>

INDEX